Willaby

By Rachel Isadora

MACMILLAN PUBLISHING CO., INC.
New York

COLLIER MACMILLAN PUBLISHERS
London

Macmillan Publishing Co., Inc.
866 Third Avenue, New York, N.Y. 10022
Collier Macmillan Canada, Ltd.
Printed in the United States of America
10   9   8   7   6   5   4   3   2   1

LIBRARY OF CONGRESS CATALOGING IN PUBLICATION DATA

Isadora, Rachel.
    Willaby.

    SUMMARY: A first grader gets into trouble when her
love of drawing keeps her from doing something important.
    [1. Drawing—Fiction] I. Title.
PZ7.I763Wi   [Fic]   77-4469
ISBN 0-02-747460-7

---

for Lisa
and Refna

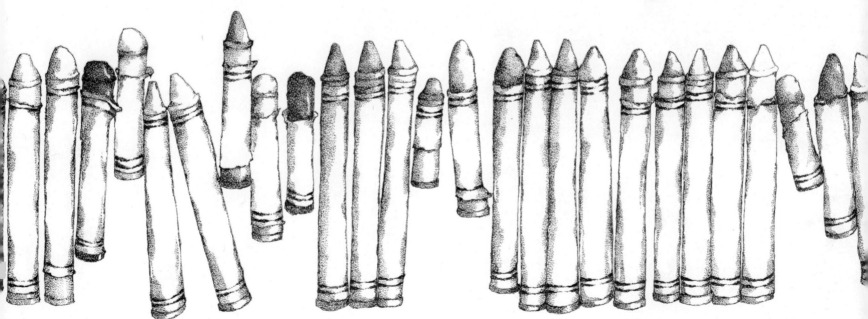

Willaby is in first grade. She likes math,
lunch, her teacher Miss Finney, and science.
But best of all Willaby likes to draw.

When the other children are playing,
Willaby is drawing.

She draws on her desk when all the others
write the history lesson in their notebooks.

ROOM 314
MISS FINNEY.

At home Willaby sometimes uses up all her paper.

Then she draws on the walls in her bedroom.

One Monday morning when Willaby goes to school, Miss Finney is not there. The substitute teacher, Mrs. Benjamin, tells the class that Miss Finney is sick and will not come back to school until the following Monday.

The class decides to send Miss Finney get-well cards. They make up
a poem and Mrs. Benjamin writes it on the blackboard.

Soon everyone is busy copying the poem. Except for Willaby.

She is busy drawing a fire truck
she saw on her way to school.

Before long Mrs. Benjamin asks the class to hand in
their cards. Willaby doesn't know what to do. She forgot all about
the get-well card and now there is no time to copy the poem.

The children put their cards in a big envelope.

On the way home from school,
Willaby suddenly remembers
she didn't sign her name
on her card!
Now Miss Finney will
never know that she sent her
a card.
Miss Finney might think she
doesn't like her.

During the week Willaby makes thirty-seven
get-well cards for Miss Finney. She signs every one.

But when Monday morning comes,
Willaby does not feel like going to school.

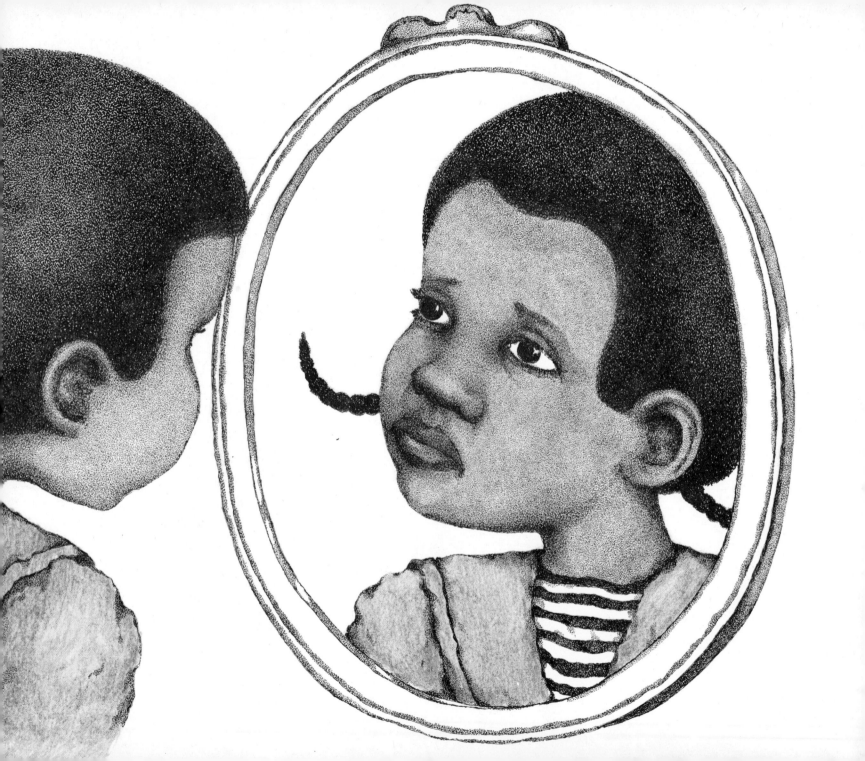

Instead of taking the bus,
she decides to walk to school.

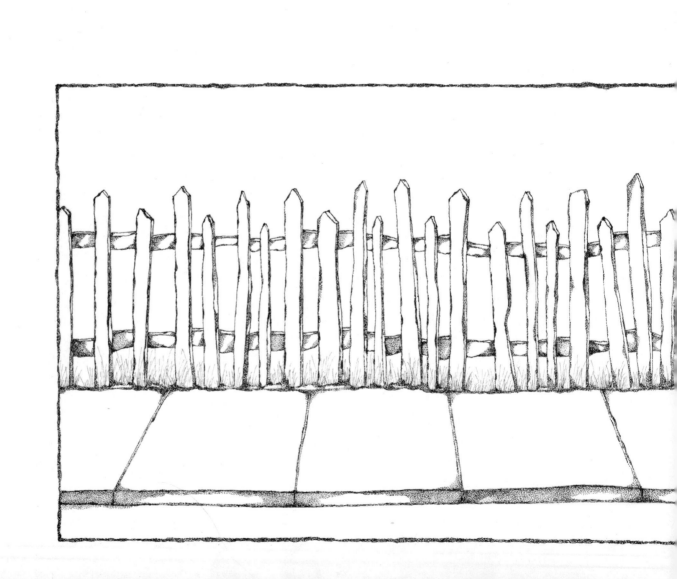

Willaby walks to her seat
without looking at Miss Finney.
But when she sits down at her desk…

Dear Willaby,
Thank you for
the get-well
picture.

Miss Finney

Willaby doesn't give Miss Finney
the thirty-seven get-well cards.
She doesn't have to!